What was India [...]
in France in [...]

Indiana Jones is that world-famous, whip-cracking hero you know from the movies....

But was he *always* cool and fearless in the face of danger? Did he *always* get mixed up in hair-raising, heart-stopping adventures?

Yes!

Read all about Indy as a kid. Join him on a quest for long-lost treasure...and come face to face with gypsies, royalty, and thieves. It's edge-of-your-seat excitement!

YOUNG INDIANA JONES

and the
GYPSY REVENGE

By Les Martin

Random House 🏠 New York

Copyright © 1991 by Lucasfilm Ltd. (LFL). All rights reserved under
International and Pan-American Copyright Conventions. Published in the
United States by Random House, Inc., New York, and simultaneously in
Canada by Random House of Canada Limited, Toronto.

Young Indy novels are conceived and produced by Random House, Inc.,
in conjunction with Lucasfilm Ltd.

Library of Congress Cataloging-in-Publication Data
Martin, Les. Young Indiana Jones and the gypsy revenge / by Les
Martin. p. cm.
Summary: In France in 1914, young Indiana Jones and his father's assistant
Thornton pursue a rare manuscript that may reveal secrets of history
involving a medieval king, mysterious gypsies, and a legendary treasure.
ISBN 0-679-81179-6 (trade)—ISBN 0-679-91179-0 (lib. bdg.)
[1. Adventure and adventurers—Fiction. 2. Gypsies—Fiction.] I. Title.
PZ7.M36353Yk 1991 [Fic]—dc20   90-52818

Manufactured in the United States of America   10 9 8 7 6 5 4 3

TM & © 1991 Lucasfilm Ltd. (LFL). All rights reserved.

Chapter 1

Young Indiana Jones's eyes widened.

The walled town in the distance looked like a picture out of a storybook. Atop the walls rose stone towers. Above them, billowing white clouds moved like great sailing ships across the deep blue sky. All that was missing from the picture were banners flapping in the strong breeze, and knights in armor riding out through the town gates.

Then the voice of the man sitting beside Indy in the carriage brought him back to the present. May of 1914.

"The walled town is Aigues-Mortes," the

man announced. "The name is Old French for 'Dead Waters.' "

His voice was dry as dust. The words came from the guidebook that Thornton N. Thornton VI was reading. He had barely lifted his eyes to give the walled town a quick glance.

That was Thornton N. Thornton VI, thought Indy with a silent groan. Buried in a book. Giving a lecture instead of talking. Thornton was twenty-two—only eight years older than Indy. But he acted as old and stuffy as Indy's dad, Professor Henry Jones. In fact, Professor Jones was Thornton's hero—just as the young history instructor was Professor Jones's most prized assistant.

That was why Indy's dad had entrusted Thornton with the mission of going to France to check out a rare medieval manuscript for him—a manuscript that the professor might very much want to buy.

The professor himself couldn't make the trip. He was to be the chief speaker at a gathering of scholars studying the Crusades. But Thornton was the perfect person to send in his place.

Thornton also was the perfect person to take Indy off his dad's hands. Professor Jones, as usual, had more important things to do than watch over his adventurous young son.

The problem was that Indy's school had ended its year early because of damage from a fire. Indy had planned to use his extra free time hunting for Indian relics in the wilds of Utah. But his dad had other ideas.

"Going to France with Thornton will be a splendid chance to further your education," he told Indy. "Thornton is the best assistant I've ever had. If anyone can rid you of your foolish, romantic notions about history, it is he."

Now, three weeks later, nearing their destination in southern France, Indy knew why his dad thought Thornton was so great.

Thornton had stayed buried in his books during the train trip to New York, their voyage across the Atlantic, their train trip from the port of Le Havre to Paris and then south to the town of Arles. A book stayed firmly in his hands as a horse-drawn carriage took them farther south on the dusty road to Aigues-Mortes, cutting though the marshland that gave the town its name. Now and then he read Indy dry pieces of information.

Thornton might just as well have never left home. He even still wore the same kind of clothes as he did back there. His tall, lean body was garbed in heavy tweeds, complete with vest, starched white shirt, and striped tie. No wonder his straw-colored hair was limp with moisture, and sweat streaked his rimless glasses.

Impatiently Thornton lifted his eyes from his book to wipe his glasses dry. Then he returned to its pages, ignoring the sight of the walled city of Aigues-Mortes coming closer.

Indy grimaced. His private nickname for Thornton N. Thornton VI summed up his opinion of his dad's favorite assistant: Thorn. He was a pain.

"Thorn," Indy remarked, "don't you ever use your eyes for anything except reading? I mean, reading's great. But there is so much more to life."

"As I've told you," Thorn replied stiffly, "my name is not Thorn. It is Thornton. It was good enough for my father, his father, his father, and the Thorntons before them.

We Thorntons are proud of being Thorntons. That is why Thornton serves as both our first name and our last. Do I make myself clear, Junior?"

"And I've told you, don't call me Junior," Indy said.

"Why?" asked Thorn, looking at Indy curiously. "That's your name, isn't it? Henry Jones, Junior. A most distinguished name. Your father, Professor Henry Jones, is the man I admire most in the world. I was honored when he entrusted you to me on this trip. And I was flattered when he said I would be a good example to you."

"Look, let's make a deal," said Indy. "I'll call you Thornton if you call me Indiana. Indy, if you're in a hurry."

Thorn thought about it. To aid his thinking, he took a pipe from his jacket pocket. He stuffed it with tobacco and lit it. Indy wrinkled his nose as the sickening smoke hit him.

Finally Thorn said, "All right. I do not want to spend valuable time in needless squabbles."

With that, Thorn returned to his guidebook. "You might find this interesting, Indiana," he said. "The population of Aigues-Mortes is currently two thousand. Its principal industries are winemaking and salt production."

Indy sighed. He had had high hopes when this trip began. But it was impossible to imagine Thornton N. Thornton VI having anything to do with adventure, danger, mystery. Or with anything else that history meant to Indy.

Then Indy took another look at the walled medieval town they were approaching.

He thought of the manuscript they were soon going to see. A manuscript found in the coffin of a mysterious corpse in knight's armor. A manuscript bearing a secret message.

Indy could only hope Thorn was wrong when Thorn complained, "Such a long way to come for such a short and dull piece of business."

Indy preferred to trust the excited thumping of his own heart to tell him what they would find behind the forbidding walls of Aigues-Mortes.

Chapter 2

Indy's hopes dimmed when he saw what the town of Aigues-Mortes was like. The narrow streets were nearly empty, the buildings old and dingy. There wasn't even a real hotel. Indy and Thorn had to settle for renting rooms above a seedy café.

"How times change," Thorn noted as they sat outside at one of the café's rickety tables. They were sipping a steaming-hot mixture of coffee and milk from large bowls. And eating rough-textured bread with delicious local honey. "Over six centuries ago, this town was filled with people. King Louis the

Ninth built it to launch his Crusade to capture the Holy Land from the Moslems. His troops crowded the streets, his ships filled the harbor."

"What harbor?" Indy said. He had seen only marshland stretching to the horizon.

Thorn took another look at his guidebook. "Over the centuries, the land around here has changed. The river Rhone once emptied into the town harbor. Gradually soil from the river filled it up, and now the sea is a full five miles from here. Aigues-Mortes as a port is history. The town is as dead as the 'Dead Waters' that gives it its name."

Indy grimaced at the smugness in Thorn's voice. Thorn liked the idea of history being nice and safe and dead. Indy had a different notion. He wanted history to come alive.

Thorn took no notice of Indy. He went on, "Yes, this place is as dead as the corpse that brings us here. That is, if there really *is* a corpse. I'll need a lot of convincing before I hand over your father's money."

Thorn patted the leather pouch on the table before him. It made a clinking noise. Inside were gold coins. Monsieur Dupont, the man they were going to see, did not trust paper money.

On the other hand, Thorn did not trust Dupont. Thorn spoke his thoughts out loud. Though Indy already knew the story of the dead knight and the mysterious manuscript, he listened keenly. The story was so weird that you had to look it over again and again, to make sure it wasn't a fake.

Thorn thought it was phony. "What a fairy tale," he said. "This Dupont fellow claims he discovered a coffin while digging an extension to his wine cellar. Inside this coffin, he finds a skeleton in knight's armor. And resting on the breastplate sits an airtight iron box. Finally, inside the box, there is a perfectly preserved manuscript."

"But why would a guy make up a story like that?" Indy asked.

"For the fortune he wants to get someone to pay for the manuscript," said Thorn. "A foolish American, of course. You notice that no French scholar would buy it."

"That's because they don't have the kind

of money Dupont wants," said Indy, remembering what his dad had told him. "The French professor who wrote my dad said it was worth a good look. He said he wished he was a rich American like my dad."

Indy had to smile at the thought. It was funny to think of his tight-fisted dad as rich. But Professor Jones actually did have quite a stash of cash. It was a legacy from a dead uncle who had hit pay dirt in the California gold rush. And though Indy's dad would walk five miles to save a nickel, no price could stop him from going after a precious piece of history.

"I'll look after your father's money as if it were my own," Thorn vowed. "There's no way Dupont will pull the wool over my eyes. I'm deeply honored your father chose me for this task. It's a golden chance to prove my worth."

The thought stirred Thorn into action. "It's time to get to work. We'll look up this Monsieur Dupont and check out his so-called medieval manuscript."

"Don't be so sure it's phony," Indy said. "It could be something really interesting.

Maybe even a treasure map. Some Crusaders came back with a lot of loot."

Thorn smiled in his irritating way. "I see why your father asked me to cure you of your romantic notions. I assure you, even if the manuscript is real, it will be a humdrum official document. A bill of sale, perhaps, or a land grant. That is the sort of thing that real historians deal with. We gather little bits of information. We are like ants working endlessly to put together a better picture of the past."

Speak for yourself, Thorn, Indy thought. As for himself, Indy would go after history in a different way. He'd be more like a big-game hunter, tracking down prize finds in faraway places.

Thorn summoned the waiter to ask the way to Dupont's house.

"You are going to see Dupont?" the waiter asked after giving them directions in heavily accented English. "Be careful of that one. He is very, very greedy. He has sold old, worthless things to foreigners for much money."

"Thank you for the advice," Thorn said, nodding. He gave Indy an I-told-you-so look.

"There is something else to be careful of," the waiter went on. *"Gitans.* You know, Gypsies."

"Gypsies? Here?" said Thorn. "Nothing in my guidebook about them."

"They come every year in May," the waiter explained, shaking his head disapprovingly. "From all over the world. They make a pilgrimage to a little fishing town thirty kilometers from here. Saintes-Maries-de-la-Mer. We have to keep a close watch on everything we own. All Gypsies are thieves."

"Thanks again," Thorn said. "Now, please, the bill."

The waiter scribbled down numbers on a small piece of paper. "That will be five francs."

Thorn looked at the paper closely. "There seems to be an error in addition. It should be two francs, forty centimes."

The waiter coughed. "Very sorry. I have this bad cold. It hurts my thinking."

Thorn and Indy left the waiter looking glumly after them as they headed for Dupont's.

Thorn, on the other hand, looked quite pleased with himself.

"I hope you're paying attention to how I do things," he told Indy. "I want you to learn the lesson: Trust no one. Always be on guard."

Indy remembered those words a few minutes later.

He would have liked to remind Thorn of them.

But by then it was too late.

Chapter 3

A girl was waiting in a small square on the way to Dupont's. She stood beside a timeworn stone statue of a crouching lion whose mouth trickled water into a cracked stone basin. The girl herself looked about twenty. She had dark hair, dark eyes, flawless olive skin, and vivid red lips. She wore gold earrings and a brightly colored blouse and skirt. Beyond a doubt, she was a Gypsy.

Indy's and Thornton's looks and clothes must have identified them just as plainly. The girl spoke to them in perfect English.

"Cross my palm with silver, and I will read

your palm," she said, and flashed them a dazzling smile.

Indy had a silver franc piece in his pocket. It was worth about twenty cents, and he was willing to blow it on a clue to his future. Indy was getting impatient for the future to arrive. Grownups got to do so much more than kids.

Before Thorn could stop him, he gave the girl the coin. She took his right hand in her two hands and studied it.

"Very interesting," she said. "You have a long, strong life line. Yet it is crossed many, many times by great danger. You will have to use your wits to survive. But one thing is certain. Your life will not be dull."

"That's sure worth a franc," Indy said.

Thorn snorted. "Can't you see that this young woman, whatever her name is, is merely telling you what any young boy wants to hear?"

The girl drew herself up straight. "My name is Sarah. And I tell the truth. If you do not believe me, let me read your palm. I will do it for nothing."

Thorn met the girl's dark eyes with his sky-blue ones. His pale skin turned pink. He cleared his throat. "Well, that is, I didn't mean—"

"Please, your palm," Sarah demanded.

Meekly Thorn extended his hand, and Sarah studied it.

Watching, Indy had to blink. All of a sudden, Thorn looked his age. Twenty-two. Or even a couple of years younger.

Sarah looked puzzled. "A strange palm. I have never seen one like it. There are so few lines on it. It is almost like a baby's. As if you have not yet begun to live."

Indy expected Thorn to look annoyed. But Thorn just kept looking into the girl's eyes.

"I'm a scholar," he told her. "That's why my hands are smooth. I don't work with them. But the work I do is quite important."

Thorn sounded odd. It was hard to know if he was apologizing or boasting. His dazed look was just as hard for Indy to figure out.

Sarah lifted her eyebrows. "A scholar? What are you doing in Aigues-Mortes?"

Thorn's voice deepened. It reminded Indy of a kid trying to sound grown-up.

"I may be purchasing a document," Thorn informed the girl. "A most valuable document. It's worth a king's ransom, in fact." To prove his words, Thorn took out the pouch filled with gold.

Indy's mouth dropped open. How could Thorn be telling this to a total stranger? And a Gypsy to boot? Had the sun scrambled his brains? Had this girl somehow hypnotized him?

"Of course, I first must decide if the document is real," Thorn went on, ignoring Indy's frantic look of warning. As far as Thorn was concerned, Indy was no longer there. Just the girl was.

"Perhaps you would like me to read my tarot cards," Sarah suggested. "They often reveal the truth."

Thorn nodded, still looking into Sarah's eyes. "That might not be a bad—"

Indy had to do something. By now he knew what was wrong with Thorn. Thorn had fallen in love.

Indy had heard about guys falling in love. But this was ridiculous. Love had come to Thornton N. Thornton VI the same way measles had hit the American Indians. Thorn clearly had no natural defenses. He was giving new meaning to the term "lovesick." It was up to Indy to provide first aid quick, before Thorn became a totally hopeless case.

"We have to get moving," Indy said loudly. "Monsieur Dupont is expecting us."

Thorn managed to snap out of it.

"I suppose he is," he agreed reluctantly. Then he said to Sarah, "Maybe we can see what the tarot says later. Where could I find you?"

"I will be in the village of Saintes-Maries," Sarah replied. "With my people. Perhaps you will be able to come there."

"Of course I can," said Thorn. "In fact, why don't we arrange a—"

"Come on," said Indy sharply. "We have to get a move on."

"Good-bye for now," Thorn said to Sarah.

"Until we meet again," she answered.

Indy waited until Thorn and he were beyond earshot. Then he said, "Hey, Thornton, do you think it was smart flashing that gold? And talking about the manuscript? After what we've heard about Gypsies?"

Thorn's stuffy, superior tone was back in full force. "That's mere popular prejudice. I'm surprised at you, listening to such nonsense. It's perfectly plain to see that Sarah is entirely honest." Then his voice softened, and a dreamy look appeared on his face. "Not only honest but understanding. Warm. Kindly. Giving. You have only to look into her eyes. Those deep, deep brown eyes. They're so—"

Indy changed the subject fast. "Well, let's hope Dupont is honest. It'd be a shame if this trip turns out to be a wild goose chase."

"It would be more of a shame to be swindled," said Thorn, coming back to the job at hand. "Believe me, I'm not opening this money sack until I get a good look at the manuscript."

It turned out Dupont had different ideas about that.

Indy and Thorn reached the address Professor Jones had provided and Thorn knocked loudly. The sign outside said that Dupont ran an antique shop. But when he opened the door, everything inside looked like junk, battered and covered with dust.

Dupont was covered with dust himself. It powdered his baggy black suit, grimy white shirt, crudely cut gray hair and walrus mustache.

The shotgun in his hands, though, was gleaming and new.

His eyes gleamed as menacingly as his gun as he said, "Hand over the money—*now*."

Chapter 4

Thorn didn't argue with the leveled gun. He handed over the money bag.

Dupont weighed it in his hand. He shook it and listened to the clinking sound. He nodded. Then he hung an Out to Lunch sign on his shop door and locked it from the inside.

"Okay. This way," he said in his primitive English. He motioned with the shotgun to a door in the rear of the shop.

Indy and Thorn went through it, with Dupont behind them. They entered a living room crammed with furniture that looked like rejects from the shop.

"Now I make sure of you," Dupont said. He held the shotgun at the ready with one hand and used his other to shake out the coins on a battered table. He picked up one and bit it. Then he stacked the coins and counted them. Finally, he nodded his head and laid aside his weapon.

"Okay. You are the Americans," he said. "One must be very careful. There are Gypsies all around here now. They will play any kind of trick to steal an honest man's goods." Dupont rubbed his sausagelike fingers together. "My goods are very good indeed. You will see."

In a corner was an old iron safe. Dupont spun the combination lock to the left, then to the right, then to the left, then to the right, and finally to the left again before it clicked. He swung open the immensely thick steel door and took out a battered metal box. He laid the box on the table and opened it. Inside were pages of yellowed paper. He put them on the table.

"The box was sealed with wax," he said. "You can see that these papers are in very good condition."

Indy craned his neck forward and squinted hard to catch a glimpse of the prize they had come so far to claim. It was strange to think that these few pages covered by tiny writing in faded ink could be worth a bag of gold.

At the same time, Thorn eagerly reached out for the manuscript to get a close look.

Dupont's hand shot out to shield it.

"Not so fast," the Frenchman said. "First you agree to pay. Then you read it. If you can. It's in a strange language. Not French."

"Probably medieval Latin," Thorn said. "Don't worry. I can read it."

"Good," said Dupont. "Now sign the bill of sale that says the money is mine."

"But I have to make sure the manuscript is genuine," Thorn insisted.

Dupont shook his head. "You take me for a fool? If you read what it says, then why buy it? No, no. First you sign."

Thorn heaved a sigh. "But it's the document that I want, not just what it says. It probably says very little, in fact. But it's a valuable artifact—if it's real."

Dupont shook his head again. "I was not born yesterday. Sign."

"Forget it. No deal," Thorn said. He reached out to take his money back. Indy had to give him credit. Thorn did have a tough side. It almost made up for the soft spot he had shown with the Gypsy girl.

Dupont bit his lip. "Fortunately, I am a reasonable man," he said. "I will let you look at a little bit of each page."

Thorn sighed, but agreed with a shrug. Dupont got a piece of cardboard from a tottering chest of drawers. He held it over most of each page that Thorn looked at. Thorn could check out only a few scattered sentences. But he saw enough to interest him as well. A sketch. Some kind of map.

"Okay, it's a deal," Thorn said. He signed the bill of sale that Dupont instantly produced.

But when Thorn reached for the manuscript, Dupont again stopped him.

"You inspected my manuscript," Dupont announced. "Now I inspect your payment. There are so many bad coins. Especially with Gypsies around."

Dupont took out a looking glass and studied a coin. Then he went on to the next.

Thorn and Indy exchanged grimaces. They had a good wait ahead of them.

At least, Indy had a chance to ask Thorn some questions. He could be sure he'd get solid answers. Thorn did know his stuff.

"So it's the real thing?" Indy said.

"Very much so," said Thorn, turning his back to Dupont. "It's even more interesting than I thought." He spoke in a low voice, though there was not much danger of Dupont's listening. Dupont was concentrating totally on the coins.

"Important?" asked Indy. "How so?"

"First, it has a date. 1270," Thorn said. "And a royal seal. The seal of Louis the Ninth. The king of France."

"Wow!" Indy exclaimed. "A king!" He looked at the manuscript with even more respect. Then he remembered something Thorn had told him. "It makes sense. Louis the Ninth—he was the guy who built this town."

"But he wasn't here in 1270," Thorn said. "He was in Africa, on his second Crusade."

"His second?" said Indy. "What happened on his first?"

"He was captured in battle in Egypt," said Thorn. "He was kept prisoner until he paid a huge ransom. But when he got back to France, he vowed to try again."

"Did he have any luck the second time?" asked Indy. This was the kind of history he liked, part adventure and part mystery.

"He had even less luck," said Thorn. "He got only as far as Tunis in North Africa. There he died of the plague. That's what makes this document so interesting. At that time, only the Moslems made linen paper like this. Louis must have sent this from North Africa back to France. One of his very last messages. A fabulous find."

"Sure is," said Indy, even more excited than Thorn. "When Dupont was turning a page, I saw a piece of a map. Maybe I was right about there being a hidden treasure."

Thorn sighed. "Indiana, *please* get rid of your romantic notions. The value of this find has nothing to do with gold or jewels. It is doubtless some kind of royal decree. As for the so-called map, it probably deals with a property dispute."

Suddenly Thorn paused, his mouth open,

his eyes thoughtful. Indy could almost hear the wheels spinning in his brain.

Thorn's eyes brightened. "I just thought of something. The knight carrying the manuscript back from North Africa must have died here of the same plague that killed Louis. That's why he was buried off by himself. They did that with plague victims."

"Hey, good thinking!" said Indy. "You wouldn't make a bad detective."

"Just part of a historian's job," said Thorn. But underneath his usual stuffy tone was a definite note of pride.

"The great part," said Indy, and picked up Thorn's train of thought. "The knight must have been sent by Louis from Tunis with this message. But he carried the plague, too. He died before he could deliver the message, and it was buried with him. Nobody opened his metal box because they were afraid to."

"It's a definite possibility," agreed Thorn. "The manuscript will tell us more."

"The manuscript is yours," Dupont declared, scooping up the money. "To show you how generous I am, I will trade this antique metal box for your leather money bag."

Indy took the box and they all traded big smiles as they said good-bye at the shop door.

"He must figure us for suckers, paying all that dough for old papers," Indy said as he and Thorn started down the narrow, deserted street. "If only he knew the truth."

"Please, restrain your imagination," Thorn said. "Remember, *we* don't know the whole truth yet."

"We soon will," said Indy. "I can hardly wait to—"

Suddenly his words were cut off by three men coming out of an alley.

The men had Gypsy mustaches and Gypsy clothes. But they were not about to tell a fortune. They were set to grab one.

Two held evil-looking Gypsy daggers. And the third pointed an even more deadly-looking pistol.

Chapter 5

The man with the pistol didn't say a word. He simply pointed his gun at the metal box.

Indy had to give Thorn credit for keeping cool. Thorn merely smiled.

"I'm afraid you're too late, my good man," Thorn said. "The gold is gone."

Thorn took the box from Indy and opened it with a smug smile. "See, just some old papers," he told the gunman. "Nothing that you would—"

That was as far as he got. One of the men with the daggers grabbed the box, while the man with the pistol kept Thorn covered.

A few minutes later, Indy and Thorn lay in the dark alleyway with gags in their mouths and ropes around their hands and feet. They watched the thieves stroll away.

Indy glared at Thorn lying beside him. He ached to give Thorn a piece of his mind. But all he could do was grunt into his grimy cloth gag. It tasted like a cross between cardboard and spinach.

How long did they have to lie here, he wondered. Probably until somebody came to pick up the garbage piled around them. In a town this empty, garbage collection might be only once a week. Of course, they could roll out into the street. But the street had been deserted. No telling when there would be a passerby.

Indy tested the ropes tying his hands and feet. They held firm. He looked around him in the alleyway for a way out of this bind. All he saw was garbage. Then amid the garbage he saw a gleam of hope.

The gleam came from an empty wine bottle. He rolled toward it. Then he turned his back to it. His hands were tied behind him, and he strained to get them on the bottle. At last, his fingers closed over its neck. With all his strength, Indy hit the bottle against the cobblestone surface of the alley.

He heard the smash of glass. It was music to his ears.

Cautiously he groped for a broken piece. When he had it, he rolled back to where Thorn lay. He hoped Thorn could figure out what he was planning to do, and help.

Thorn lay like a log, with a puzzled look in his eyes.

Indy sighed to himself. But he wasn't surprised. Getting out of trouble clearly was not Thorn's specialty—getting into it was.

Indy grunted as loud as he could as he shoved against Thorn, trying to get Thorn to roll onto his side.

Finally, Thorn got the idea. Then Indy inched over to lie back to back with him. At last, Indy was able to use the jagged glass to saw away at the rope around Thornton's hands.

Back and forth, back and forth, the jagged glass went. Bead after bead of sweat popped up on Indy's skin and dripped down it. His clothes were soaked, and his wrist was about to give out, when he felt the glass cut clean through the rope.

Thorn's hands were free. Indy rolled over onto his back, breathing heavily, while Thorn finished untying himself. Seconds later, Thorn took off Indy's gag, then set to work on the ropes.

"Think you can manage the knots?" Indy asked.

"Of course I can," Thornton said. "I was an Eagle Scout." He swiftly undid Indy's hands and feet. "I memorized the merit badge manual for knots."

Leave it to Thorn to get his survival skills from books, Indy thought. Then his mind turned to more pressing matters.

"Now let's get back the manuscript," he said. "It's a good thing we know who took it."

Thorn looked puzzled. "What do you mean? I never saw those thugs before. Did you?"

"I don't have to know who those guys are," Indy said. "Not when I know who got them to go after us."

"I still don't understand," said Thorn.

"You mean, you don't *want* to under-stand," Indy told him. "You know as well as I do that the Gypsy girl, Sarah, was the only one who knew about the money you were carrying. And if that isn't proof enough, she definitely was the only one who knew that the manuscript was worth anything. I still can't believe you told her so much, so fast."

"Sarah? A criminal?" Thorn said, shocked. He shook his head firmly. "Impossible. One glance at her, and I could see she was the soul of innocence. I'd bet my life on it."

"You already did, and almost lost," Indy commented. "Now what's at stake is my dad's manuscript. The manuscript you promised to bring back to him."

"And I will," Thorn declared. He drew his tall body up to full height, like a flagpole with a proud banner. "A Thornton always does his duty."

"Then a Thornton has to face the fact that Sarah is the main suspect," Indy said.

"Well . . ." said Thorn. He bit his lower lip. Then he took off his glasses, wiped them with a handkerchief, and put them on again. His eyes refused to meet Indy's.

"We have to go to the cops and tell them about her," Indy insisted.

"I still can't believe—" Thorn began.

"You don't have to," said Indy. "You can let the law decide. She'll get a fair trial."

Thorn shook his head. "Will she? There's so much prejudice against Gypsies. Besides, Sarah is very young. Even if she was somehow involved, doubtless she was forced into it. We must give her a chance to clear her name, or at least give back the manuscript, before her whole life is ruined." Thorn nodded firmly, his mind made up. "Yes. That is what we must do. Go to Saintes-Maries and see Sarah."

One look at the stubborn set of Thorn's jaw, and Indy gave up the thought of arguing any more. All he could do was insist, "And if there's no Sarah at Saintes-Maries, we go to the cops."

Thorn bit his lips again. "Agreed," he said. "It's a gamble I'm willing to take."

Thorn taking a gamble, Indy thought. After this, nothing could surprise him.

But Indy was wrong. The surprises were just beginning.

Chapter 6

"Think how impressive it will look. Us driving into Saintes-Maries in a car," Indy told Thorn. Indy was trying to get Thorn to go along with his brainstorm. Indy had spotted a garage in Aigues-Mortes with a car in front of it for rent. An open-top Renault. Indy was aching to see how it compared with the Model T Ford he had learned to drive back home.

"A horseless carriage?" said Thorn. "Quite out of the question. Those things are little more than toys. A passing fad. Plus there's all the noise they make and the fumes they give off. It's a disgusting way to travel."

Indy decided to play his ace in the hole. "There are so few cars around here. Think how Sarah's eyes will pop out when she sees it. If she's hiding, it might lure her out of cover—just from curiosity."

"One can't really be sure of that," Thorn said, but his firm tone was wavering.

Indy gave another push. "Why, she might even want to take a spin with us. In fact, I bet she will."

"There might be certain advantages," Thorn admitted. Then his face clouded. "There *is* one little problem, though. I don't know how to drive. Of course, the car must come with a manual. All I'd have to do is read it and—"

"No problem," Indy cut in very quickly. "I've been practicing driving all winter."

"But you're too young," Thorn said. "Surely there are laws."

"I doubt it," said Indy. "Cars are so new around here. Besides, finding Sarah is worth a little risk. Don't you agree?"

That did it. Thorn gave a determined nod. "It's worth a lot of risk."

Indy winced. Thorn was a goner where

Sarah was concerned. Indy had to keep a close eye on him. He had to save Thorn from his own weakness.

One thing he couldn't save. His dad's money. His dad had given Thorn a generous amount for travel expenses and to cover anything extra Dupont might demand. Until now, Thorn had been watching every penny. But when it came to seeing Sarah again, suddenly money was no object. Thorn didn't make a peep of protest about the car rental price that the garage owner demanded. He simply shoved the money into the man's hand.

The owner's mouth dropped open. Then he broke into a warm smile. All the stories about rich and crazy Americans were true. In fact, he had a story of his own now. About how the American boy instead of the man got behind the wheel.

The owner shrugged. The rental fee, plus the deposit he demanded, would buy him two cars. He cheerfully cranked the car to start it and gave a warm farewell wave as Indy and Thorn drove away in the open-top Renault.

Indy was pleased that the Renault made almost as good time as the Model T Ford. Aigues-Mortes disappeared behind them. After a few miles, it began to look as if they had left France as well.

The road cut through swampy grassland as far as the eye could see. Indy was startled to make out men on horseback in the distance. And herds of cattle.

"Cowboys," Indy said. "What are they doing here?"

Thorn consulted his faithful guidebook. "They're called *gardians*. They do a lot of cattle raising in this region, the Camargue."

Looking more closely, Indy could see that these men wore flat-topped, wide-brimmed hats, not Stetsons. Their mounts were smaller than American horses, and white. And they carried long sticks with three prongs on the ends.

But they were definitely cowboys. They had lassos coiled on their saddle horns, leathery faces tanned dark by the sun, and lean, hard bodies that seemed part of their horses. Indy got a good look at the cattle, too—hundreds of them, with long, mean-looking horns.

"Wait until I tell them about this back home," Indy said. "The Wild West in the south of France."

"A little *too* wild," Thorn said. "It looks like we're going to be stalled here for a while."

Streams of cattle, with *gardians* prodding them along, were pouring across the road in front of them. It was ten minutes before the last few cows straggled by.

Indy sighed. He wished somebody would get around to inventing an automatic starter for cars. But right now, the only way to start a car was to insert a crank in the front and give it a few sharp turns to spark the motor into life. And the garage owner wasn't around to do that favor for them here in the middle of nowhere.

"I'm afraid you have to get out and crank us up, Thornton," Indy said.

He should have known Thorn's answer. It was as plain as the spotless white suit Thorn was wearing. There was no way Thorn would risk soiling the shining picture he wanted to present to Sarah.

"You crank the car," Thorn told him.

"But nobody will be at the wheel when the engine starts," Indy protested.

"I'll be there," Thorn declared.

"But you don't know anything about driving," Indy pointed out.

"Nonsense," Thorn said. "I've watched you. There's nothing to it. Child's play."

Indy sighed again. "Okay. But remember, you don't have to do anything. I'll crank her up and hop right back into the driver's seat."

Reluctantly Indy got out. He inserted the crank in the front of the car and gave it a hard turn. The engine came to life. Instantly. Ten times faster than the Ford back home. Indy was thrown off balance. He couldn't make it back to the driver's seat in time.

He stood helplessly by, the crank dangling in his hand, as the car lurched into motion. Thorn must have been fiddling around with the gears. All Indy could do was yell, "The brake, Thornton, the brake!"

"Brake? Where's the bra—?" Thornton shouted as the car headed off the road and into the swamp, where it came to a slow stop.

Thorn got out of the car and waded back

onto the road. He looked down at his pants legs. They were dripping with green slime.

"I guess I must have pushed the wrong thingamajig," he said.

"I guess so," agreed Indy.

"And I guess there's not much chance of starting the car again," Thorn said, glancing behind him.

"I guess not," said Indy. The car was half submerged. The motor would need a total overhaul.

Then Indy brightened. "But we still have a chance to get to Saintes-Maries. Look."

Four *gardians* were riding down the road toward them. They had spotted the accident.

"Any money left?" Indy asked Thorn.

"Quite a bit," said Thorn.

"Is your French good enough to rent a couple of their horses?" asked Indy. "And to get the car hauled back to Aigues-Mortes?"

"I should say so," said Thorn. "I studied French for ten years."

"Then we're in business," Indy said.

He was right, even though Thorn's French wasn't quite as good as he thought it was.

Writing a paper on the French Revolution wasn't the same as making a deal with French cowboys. But the money that Thorn flashed spoke loud and clear.

Thorn and Indy were left in charge of two horses. The *gardians* used the others to haul the car out of the swamp and down the road back to its owner. When Thorn and Indy were finished with their mounts, they'd leave them in a stable in Aigues-Mortes. The *gardians* could pick them up there.

"Maybe it's worked out for the best," Indy told Thorn. "It'll really impress Sarah, your riding up on a white charger."

Thorn lit up like an electric bulb. "Time to saddle up," he said. "Let's go!"

Suddenly a thought hit Indy.

"Hey, Thornton, you ever ridden a—?"

He was too late. Thorn had already managed to hoist himself into the saddle.

A moment later, Thornton was holding on for dear life, desperately shouting "Stop, horse, stop!"

The horse had never studied English. It galloped off, totally out of control.

Chapter 7

Indy watched Thorn's horse racing away. Then he looked at his own horse, and saw a lasso looped in the saddle horn.

Indy hadn't grown up in the West for nothing. He knew how to use a lasso. But watching old cowhands and practicing on tame cattle was one thing—this was something else. Indy swung up onto his horse, and raced after Thorn.

Minutes later, he was in range.

"Go for it," Indy said to himself, and the lasso whistled through the air.

"Bingo!" he said as the loop settled over the neck of Thorn's mount.

Indy barely had to give a yank. The feel of the rope seemed to bring Thorn's horse to its senses. Maybe it remembered other lassos around its neck, when it was being trained.

Whatever the reason, it came to a quick halt. It stood still, its flanks heaving, as Indy rode to its side. Thorn was breathing hard too. But at least he *was* breathing.

Somehow he had stayed in the saddle. He was blinking in a dazed way. His glasses were dangling from one ear. His hair had lost its neat part down the center and was sticking up like a straw-colored mop. The longer this trip went on, the less Thorn looked like Thornton N. Thornton VI.

"Hey, I don't expect applause," Indy said with a grin, "but how about a little thank-you?"

Thorn cleared his throat. "Yes, of course. Thank you, Indiana. Though actually I was beginning to get the hang of riding. A few more minutes, and I would have mastered it."

Indy shook his head. Thorn may have

changed on the outside, but inside he was definitely still Thorn.

Then Indy sniffed the air. He caught a sea scent. Up the road a tall church tower rose above the horizon.

"Think that's Saintes-Maries?" Indy asked. He half expected Thorn to declare he had pointed the horse the right way on purpose.

But Thorn was still too shaken up. "I think so," was all he said.

"Maybe we ought to walk the rest of the way," Indy suggested.

Thorn, white-faced, nodded. He slid off his mount even more awkwardly than he had hoisted himself up.

Indy dismounted too. Leading the horses, they trudged up the dusty road. On both sides, pools of water in the marshland shimmered like pools of blood in the setting red sun.

Soon they reached the town—what there was of it. Saintes-Maries was a long, narrow street lined with shabby houses and shops. All were dwarfed by a huge old stone church.

"Looks more like a fort than a church,"

said Indy, looking up at the massive structure.

Thorn already had his guidebook out of his
pocket. His voice returned to normal as he
read from it.

"In part, it was," he said. "It was built to
defend against attacks of pirates from North
Africa. They ravaged the coast. But still, it
was a church. An important one."

"Here, in this tiny place?" wondered Indy.

"Legend said that a boat from the Holy
Land landed here," Thorn explained. "On it
were three saints, all with the first name of
Mary. Of course, 'Mary' in French is 'Marie.' "

"Saintes-Maries. I get it," said Indy. "Is
that why the Gypsies make their big pilgrimage here? Is one of those Marys their
patron saint or something?"

"Let's see," said Thorn. He turned a page.
His eyes lit up. His voice was no longer dry
as he said, "There was an Egyptian servant
girl with the saints. She's the one the Gypsies
took as their saint."

"What was her name?" Indy asked. But
he could almost guess the answer from the
tremor in Thorn's tone, the glow in his eyes.

"Sarah," Thorn said. Then he added "Come on. Let's find the Gypsy camp."

It was easy to do. The town street ended on a long, wide white sand beach. It was covered by hundreds of Gypsy caravans. They were the Gypsies' living quarters on wheels, drawn by the horses now tied beside them.

"What a mob scene," said Indy. "All these Gypsies in one place. How are we going to find Sarah?"

"There has to be a way," Thorn said. There was no mistaking the look in his eyes. Thorn was going to get to see Sarah again even if it meant checking through the vast throng of Gypsies one by one.

They walked among the caravans and cooking fires. Children swarmed around them, asking for coins. Women swarmed around them, offering to tell their fortune. But the men were the most pressing. They shouted offers to buy or trade the horses that Thorn and Indy were leading. No one—man, woman, or child—took no for an answer.

"We'll have to keep an eye on the horses," said Indy. "You know what they say about Gypsies. They're known as the world's greatest horse thieves, and trickiest horse dealers."

Thorn shot him a disapproving look. "I'm surprised at you, Indiana. Shocked, in fact. You shouldn't listen to that kind of talk. Groups of people who are slightly different are always victims of unjust prejudice. You're old enough to know that by now."

"Sorry, I wasn't thinking," Indy said, deciding that Thorn had become one of the world's leading Gypsy defenders. Actually, it seemed to do him good. There was a fire in his eyes, a strength in his stride that Indy had never seen before. If love could do that, maybe it wasn't all bad. Still, Indy reminded himself, it was up to him to keep an eye out for both Thorn and himself as far as Sarah was concerned. Whatever else love might be for Thorn, it was also definitely blind.

Meanwhile, Thorn was intently scanning the faces lit by the Gypsy fires on the beach. By now the sun had almost dipped below the sea. The sea was lavender, the sky deep purple. Night was falling. Time to find Sarah was running out.

In desperation, Thorn finally spoke to a man who persisted in clutching at his elbow. "Tell me, my good man, do you happen to know a young lady named Sarah?"

"Sarah?" The man flashed them a gold-toothed grin. "We have hundreds of girls named Sarah. But we have very few horses as fine as the ones I will trade you for your old nags. Only because I have this terrible weakness for white horses. It will be the ruin of me."

Thorn impatiently turned away from him. Then he froze.

Indy followed his gaze. There, dancing alone before a bonfire, was Sarah.

It was a whirling, foot-stomping Spanish dance—done to the harsh strumming of a guitar player standing in the shadows, and the sharp clicks of castanets flashing in Sarah's hands. Thorn watched spellbound. Indy had to admit, Sarah was good.

Then, with a sudden twang of the guitar and a decisive stamp of Sarah's feet, the dance was over. Before Thorn and Indy could make a move toward Sarah, she came to them.

"You're here," she said, looking into Thorn's eyes. "That's wonderful. Tomorrow I was going to hunt for you."

"Really?" said Thorn, in the sappy tone that Sarah brought out in him. "More of my fortune you wanted to tell?"

Sarah shook her head. "No. There's someone you have to see. Someone who wants to hear what *you* have to tell."

"Who is he?" Thorn asked.

"You'll see," Sarah said. "I'll take you to him now."

Thorn was all set to go off with Sarah. Indy had to slow him down. He had to keep Thorn from walking into what could be a trap.

"You're not going to leave me here alone with the horses?" he said, making himself sound scared. "A little kid like me? With all these Gypsies around? Remember, you promised my dad you'd watch out for me."

Thorn hesitated, his eyes flickering between Sarah and Indy.

Indy waited for Sarah to come up with a way to make Thorn do what she wanted. Indy tried to think of a way to keep Thorn out of her clutches.

But Sarah didn't have to do a thing. Another Gypsy did it for her. A very large Gypsy, with a gold earring on one ear, and a glittering knife in his hand. With him was another Gypsy, just as big, his knife just as menacing.

"You and the boy, come with us," the first man said.

"But the horses," Indy protested with a sinking feeling.

"Don't worry about them," the man said. "We Gypsies are very good at taking care of horses."

"And at taking care of gorgios who do not listen to reason," his companion added.

Neither Thorn nor Indy had to ask what "gorgios" were.

The hard looks and drawn knives said it all.

"Gorgios" were "outsiders." Gorgios were them.

Chapter 8

The man waiting for Indy and Thorn in his caravan was old, very old. His head was bald, except for a fringe of white hair around his ears. His full beard and mustache were white, and his swarthy face was crisscrossed with lines of age. But his dark eyes were bright and keen. Indy could almost feel the old man's gaze cutting into him.

"This is my great-grandfather Stefan," Sarah said. "He wants to hear about the old manuscript you came to buy. The one you told me about."

Sarah stood beside Indy and Thorn in the caravan. No one else was present. But outside, the two men with knives stood guard, along with two others who had been there when they arrived.

Stefan sat on a large, beautifully embroidered royal-blue silk cushion. To Indy it looked like a Gypsy throne. Then there was the old man's air of command, and the respect he was shown. Indy figured he might as well say what he was thinking. He didn't see that Thorn and he had much to lose.

"Before we tell you anything, you should tell us something. Who you are," Indy said, ignoring Thorn's efforts to shush him. "But maybe I can guess. I once read a book about Gypsies. It talked about a Gypsy king."

Indy half expected the old man to be annoyed at his probing. But Stefan merely smiled.

"Doubtless the book was written by a gorgio," Stefan said. "Outsiders have many strange ideas about us. The truth is that the Rom have no king."

"The Rom?" said Indy.

"That is what we call ourselves. Or else Romanies. Or Romanichels."

"What about 'Gypsies'?" Indy asked.

"That is the name that gorgios gave us, when we first came to Europe," Stefan explained. "It is short for 'Egyptians.' You see, the first of our people to come here arrived from Egypt. And gorgios made the first of their mistakes about us."

"Then if the Gyp—" Indy stopped himself. "If the Rom didn't come from Egypt, where did they come from originally?"

The old man shrugged. "Who knows? There are many stories," he said vaguely. Then his voice grew sharp. "But now it is your turn to tell me a few things. I want to hear about this manuscript you were buying."

Indy shot Thorn a warning glance, telling him to keep his mouth shut. But Sarah turned her dark eyes on Thorn at the same time.

"Please, tell Stefan all you know," she said softly. "It is very important."

Indy had to act fast, before Thorn caved in. "Why do you want to know?" he demanded of Stefan. "To find out how much your loot is worth?"

"What is he talking about?" Sarah asked Thorn.

"I hate to tell you, but three Gyp—" It was Thorn's turn to stop himself. "Three Rom stole the manuscript from us at gunpoint."

Sarah shook her head in denial. Stefan's response was even firmer. "I assure you no Rom stole your manuscript."

Indy's eyes lit up. "Are you sure?"

"Of *course* I am. *I* would know if one of my people did such a thing." Stefan declared.

Indy had caught the old man in his little trap. "*How* would you know? I mean, if you're not a king or anything?"

"Indy!" Thorn said sharply. "You must learn to show some respect to your elders."

But Stefan didn't get angry at Indy. His eyes crinkled with amusement. And a bit of approval at Indy's persistence. "Let's say our people are very close-knit," he said. "We have no secrets from one another."

"Then who were the guys who robbed us?" Indy said. "They wore Gypsy clothes." He paused. The word "Gypsy" had slipped out. He apologized. "I'm sorry. It's hard for me not to say 'Gypsy.'"

"Don't apologize," Stefan said gently.

"There is nothing wrong with the word. It is part of your language. What is wrong is what gorgios think about that word. To them it means a thief. That is why many real thieves dress up in our clothes. It is so easy to throw the blame for their crimes on us."

"Yes, that must have been what happened," Thorn declared, and was rewarded by a warm look from Sarah.

This spurred Thorn on. "We'll go to the police immediately and report the crime."

Stefan shook his head. "That would not be wise. You might believe the Rom are innocent. But the police would not. They, too, think Gypsies are thieves. They would sweep through our camp. They would arrest many of us. It has happened before."

"Then what can we do?" Thorn wondered. "I have to get the manuscript back. It is very important to me."

"It is to us as well," Stefan said.

Indy looked at him curiously. "Why?" he asked.

Stefan kept a poker face. "Why, to clear our name, of course. We don't want even a hint of suspicion to fall on the Rom." Then he spoke to Thorn. "Our people will fan out over the countryside. We will try to find clues to the crime. Meanwhile, you can go back to Aigues-Mortes and do you own investigation." Stefan smiled. "I will send Sarah with you to help. She and you seem to get on so well together."

Indy had to hand it to the old man. Stefan knew how to play his cards. Thorn's face lit up "What a splendid idea," he said. "We'll get to the bottom of this in no time. We'll saddle up and head back to Aigues-Mortes first thing in the morning. That is, if you have a horse and know how to ride, Sarah."

"I am a Rom," she said. "Of course I do."

Indy thought of Thorn's riding skills. He cleared his throat. "We'll have to be careful not to go too fast. We don't want to return our horses worn out."

Thorn gave Indy a sheepish look. Then he said, "Quite right. A good rider always takes care of his mount."

Indy grinned at Thorn. Inwardly he gave a sigh of relief. At least, Thorn would get back to Aigues-Mortes in one piece.

But where would things go from there?"

Indy's eyes narrowed. He still had to watch out for tricks, traps, and trouble. He could see that Stefan was using Sarah to lead Thorn by the nose. But why?

Chapter 9

Before they set out for Aigues-Mortes the next morning, Sarah insisted on reading her tarot cards to see what was waiting for them there. Indy joined Thorn in watching closely. He didn't know whether it was safe to trust Sarah or not. But it was clear that Thorn trusted her completely and absolutely. Indy knew one way to be sure Sarah didn't try anything—he was going to stick to Thorn like glue whenever the Gypsy girl was around.

She shuffled the deck of cards seven times. Then she laid ten cards facedown to form a pyramid.

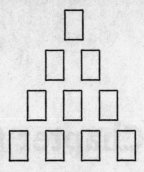

One by one, she turned over the cards in the bottom three rows of the pyramid. She bit her lip.

"Most unusual," she said. "They are all swords."

"Swords?" asked Indy.

"There are four suits in tarot cards—wands, pentacles, cups, and swords," Sarah explained.

"Is that good or bad?" Thorn asked.

"Swords can be a force for good or evil," Sarah replied, still looking intently at the cards. "It depends on whether they are right side up or upside down. Upside down is called 'reversed.'"

Indy looked at the cards. "They're *all* reversed. I guess that's not so good."

"You're right," said Sarah. "But it depends on the card at the top. That's the card that commands the others—and holds them together."

She turned that last card faceup.

"A man with a crown," said Thorn.

"With a sword in his hand," said Indy.

"And reversed," said Sarah grimly.

"More bad news?" asked Indy.

"I'm afraid so. The king of swords reversed," said Sarah. "We're facing more than a simple gang of thieves. We're facing an army of evil. And it is led by a man who is cruel, cunning, and very ambitious. He will stop at nothing to get what he wants."

"He's already gotten what he wants," said Thorn. "Now it's up to us to get him."

Indy kept quiet. Thorn had swallowed Sarah's story about the cards hook, line, and sinker. But Indy wasn't so sure. The odds of cards falling that way had to be one in a million. Sarah could have done a fast shuffle with a stacked deck. She had to want Thorn to believe that some kind of spooky bad guy had stolen the manuscript. A bad guy who wasn't a Gypsy.

Actually, Sarah didn't look like a Gypsy

now. She had changed out of her Gypsy clothes and looked like an ordinary French village girl. That just made Indy resolve to keep an even closer eye on her. She seemed to know a lot about deception and disguise.

Indy had to admit one thing, though. Sarah had told the truth about being able to ride a horse. She sat in the saddle beautifully as they rode toward Aigues-Mortes.

Watching her, even Thorn managed to sit tall—tall for him, anyway. In fact, he didn't look too bad. His white suit had lost its crease and developed a nice set of wrinkles and streaks of grime. It looked as if it belonged to a man of action instead of a stuffed shirt. And for the first time on the trip, Thorn had removed his tie. It was Thorn's way of stripping for action, Indy supposed.

At Aigues-Mortes, Thorn and Indy left their mounts in a stable for the *gardians* to pick up. Sarah left hers there as well. A Gypsy would come by for it later.

Indy grinned to himself, watching Thorn try not to wince as he walked. Thorn didn't want Sarah to suspect what the ride had done to his thigh muscles. He wanted Sarah to see him at his best. And as far as Thorn was concerned, the best part of him was his brain.

"We have to use logic," he said. "The thieves knew we had the manuscript, and knew it was valuable. Only Dupont could have told them that. He, or someone he talked to. We have to go to Dupont and get a list of everyone who knew about the manuscript."

"Hey, maybe it was Dupont himself who hired the thieves," Indy said. "He figured he'd sell the manuscript to us, then steal it back. Have his cake and eat it too. I wouldn't put it past him. He's one greedy character."

Thorn nodded. "Maybe so. We'll keep that in mind when we pay Dupont a visit." He turned to Sarah. "What do you think?"

"I think you are absolutely right—and very smart," she said.

Thorn turned pink, cleared his throat, and went on, "Thinking clearly is part of my profession. Now let's be off to Dupont's."

"I hope we can get him to talk," Indy said. "He's our only lead."

"I'm sure he will," Thorn replied. "I've got

enough money left to loosen his tongue."

"If that doesn't do it," said Indy, "we can be pretty sure Dupont himself is guilty. Either way, we'll be a step closer to cracking this case."

They turned down the street to Dupont's. It wasn't deserted now. Townspeople, young and old, male and female, were going in the same direction as they were. They had eager expressions on their faces. It was as if a circus had come to town.

"I wonder what's up," said Indy.

"Look at that crowd, right in front of Dupont's," said Thorn. He quickened his step. "Let's see what's going on."

They reached the edge of the crowd. Indy stood on tiptoe and craned his neck to get a look through a gap in the wall of people in front of him. He saw a couple of French police guarding the door of Dupont's shop.

At the same time, Thorn spied the waiter who worked at their café-hotel. Thorn elbowed his way through the crowd to reach him, with Indy and Sarah close behind.

"What's happened?" Thorn asked.

"It is terrible! Horrible!" the waiter declared. "Someone like Monsieur Dupont. A respectable citizen. A good businessman. But he was, I must say, a bit foolish. He kept boasting how much he had sold his manuscript for. The champagne he had drunk to celebrate loosened his tongue."

"But what happened?" Thorn asked again.

"What kind of world is this?" the waiter went on. "A man cannot be safe in his own home. Oh, those Gypsies. They spread over here like a plague. Let us hope the law now brings them to justice. Or else we must take the law into our own hands."

"Did something happen to Monsieur Dupont?" Indy said, to cut the man's speech short.

The man answered with a grim gesture. He drew his finger across his throat. "In his own shop. The Gypsies will pay for this."

Thorn, Indy, and Sarah looked at one another. Without a word, they walked away from the scene of the crime.

"Looks like we've hit a dead end," Thorn said glumly.

But Sarah had a more pressing concern.

"I must warn my people," she said. "They

will have to stay off the streets for a while. This kind of thing has happened before. There is a crime. We are blamed for it. And local people turn ugly."

"I see now why you changed out of your Gypsy clothes," Indy said. "Wearing them can be dangerous."

"Yes, sometimes," Sarah agreed.

She was not the only one who thought so. The three men who came up beside Indy, Thorn, and Sarah clearly thought the same way.

They were no longer wearing Gypsy clothes. They no longer flourished Gypsy knives. Their Gypsy mustaches were gone. Even their swarthy coloring had faded.

But Indy recognized them right away. It was easy. He just had to see the pistol in their leader's hand.

Chapter 10

Not a word was spoken. None was needed. The pistol shoved into Thorn's side said it all.

The thieves herded Sarah, Indy, and Thorn to the edge of town. There a car was waiting. The man with the gun got in the back with them, and his companions got in the front. The car started off.

Indy began to say something to Thorn. But he had barely opened his mouth when the pistol was pointed right into it. Indy got the message. The rest of the ride passed in silence.

Indy looked out the window. They were rolling through the cattle country of the Camargue again. The car left the main road. It bounced along a side road that was little more than a path.

Indy's brain was buzzing. Why had these crooks come after them? The answer was easy: The crooks figured that by now Indy and Thorn must have told the cops they had been robbed by Gypsies. Now Indy and Thorn would disappear. That way they couldn't be asked to identify the Gypsies the law rounded up. Those Gypsies would land in jail. And the real crooks would get away free.

Usually Indy was pleased when he came up with an answer to a puzzle. But not this time. All his brainwork did was tell him what waited for them at the end of the ride.

It would be a dead end.

And he couldn't think of any way to head it off.

The car braked to a halt. The gunman motioned for Indy, Thorn, and Sarah to get out. Indy gulped. He saw Thorn swallow hard as well. Thorn was thinking the same thing Indy was. From Sarah's scared look, so was she.

The car was parked next to a small hut. There was no other human dwelling in sight—only empty marshland, desolate in the dying daylight. There was no one to hear gunshots, and lots of room for unmarked graves.

There was another car, though. A long black car. It had a uniformed chauffeur in the driver's seat, and curtains cutting off a view of the backseat.

Indy knew of only one kind of long black limousine like that. The kind used to carry corpses. A hearse.

Maybe that meant they wouldn't be buried here. Maybe there was an even safer place to dispose of their bodies.

One of the crooks opened the door of the hut. The man with the gun motioned his captives inside.

Indy bit his lip. Would they be killed inside the hut? To stifle the gunshot? That must be it. The crooks were afraid a *gardian* might be near enough to hear. Indy's stomach sank as he went into the hut with Thorn and Sarah.

The hut was sparsely furnished. There was a narrow bed, a battered trunk, wall hooks for clothes, and a table with three chairs. It was probably a *gardian*'s hut, thought Indy, spotting a battered *gardian*'s hat on a hook. Maybe the owner would come back in the nick of time—but somehow Indy didn't think so. The crooks had probably removed that risk. Indy didn't want to think of what might have happened to the *gardian*. These crooks didn't look as if they took prisoners.

Then Indy's gaze fastened on the table. And everything else was forgotten.

There were no windows in the hut. The only light came from an oil lamp on the table. That lamp shone bright on the old manuscript that lay beside it.

Thorn saw it too. He rushed to it. No one made a move to stop him. In fact, a smile appeared on the gunman's face.

As Thorn eagerly inspected the manuscript the gunman nodded to one of his companions. The man opened the hut door and gave a signal with his hand.

Thorn didn't notice. He was too immersed

in the manuscript. Sarah seemed as fascinated as Thorn was. She stood behind him, looking down intently.

"Is that it?" she asked him.

"Yes, it is," Thorn said. "Now I understand what's going on. The thieves have figured out how hard it is to sell. They want me to buy it back."

Sarah nodded. There was hope on her face now, just as there was on Thorn's.

But Indy barely heard Thorn's words. He was watching the crook moving away from the doorway to make room for someone to enter.

Then Indy saw the man who walked in.

"Thorn! Sarah! Look!" Indy said.

They did.

The manuscript was forgotten in the shock of the sight that greeted their eyes.

A tall man dressed entirely in black stood in the doorway. Black suit, black shirt, black tie, black shoes.

But what was truly startling was his face. Or rather, what covered his face.

It was a mask. A black mask—with slits

for the eyes and a breathing hole for the nose and another slit for the mouth.

But it was not an ordinary mask. Not a mask of cloth or paper or even wood.

It was a mask of metal. An iron mask.

Chapter 11

The man in the iron mask spoke excellent English, with a strong French accent. His voice was smooth and assured.

"I see you can read the manuscript, Mr. Thornton," he said. "Congratulations. Such scholarship is rare. People today are so concerned with new things, they neglect the treasures of the past."

"You know my name?" Thorn said.

"For a few francs, the innkeeper was happy to show me his guest list," the man in the iron mask responded.

"Since you know who I am, let's get down to business," Thorn said. "You may think all

Americans are rich, but I assure you, my funds are limited. Still, I am prepared to make you an offer for the manuscript—if you are not too greedy."

The man found this funny. He shook with silent laughter. Then he said, "You have it wrong. It is I who am making *you* an offer. For your services."

"My services?" said Thorn.

"I want you to translate this manuscript," the man explained. "Dupont did not tell me it was in medieval Latin. He doubtless did not know it himself. Dupont was an idiot. Only an idiot would refuse my offer to buy his find just because he had agreed to sell it to an American. Of course, Dupont kept insisting he was an honest businessman. As I said, he was a fool. I hope for your sake that you are not one too."

"What gives you the idea *I* would help *you*?" said Thorn with scorn.

Indy looked at him with new respect. Thorn did have backbone. At least when it came to selling out his precious learning.

But the man in the iron mask sounded as if he was smiling. "I don't think you will want to ignore my offer," he said. "If you do what I say, I will let you keep your life."

Indy couldn't keep quiet any longer. He had been putting two and two together, and wanted Thorn to know what it added up to.

"Why should he believe you?" Indy said to the man in the iron mask. "You killed Dupont because he could connect you to the theft of the manuscript. You'd do the same to Thornton as soon as he helped you." Indy turned to Thorn. "You can't make a deal with a killer."

It was Thorn's turn to look at Indy with respect. "Quite right." Then he said to the man in the iron mask, "No deal."

The man's voice was icy. "If you don't care about your own life, think of the boy's."

"Don't listen to him," Indy pleaded. "I'm in the same boat you are. I know too much to live."

Thorn nodded grimly.

But the man in the iron mask had another card to play.

"Then think of this girl," he said. "Her dress does not fool me. I know she is a Gypsy. And that means it would be safe for me to let her live. Even if she went to the police, they would not believe her. Not that she would. Gypsies do not care about anyone but their own kind. So I will let her go—*if* you cooperate."

Indy looked at Sarah. Maybe she would tell Thorn not to listen.

Sarah stayed silent. She refused to meet Indy's eyes. Indy sighed to himself. He should have known. Sarah was saving her own skin. Or maybe she was even in cahoots with the crooks. Maybe the iron mask hid a Gypsy face. Indy did not want to think that—but right now he did not know what to think.

He saw Thorn look at Sarah too. Sarah did meet his gaze. Thorn's firm expression melted. Indy knew what his decision would be. Thorn would do anything on the chance of saving Sarah.

"Okay. I'll give you your translation." Thorn turned to the manuscript. Slowly he began to read aloud.

An hour later, he had finished his job. He laid aside the last page of the manuscript. Silence filled the hut. Everyone was trying to digest the story that the manuscript told.

It was written by King Louis IX—written in Tunis, North Africa, where the French king had landed to begin his second Crusade. And where he lay dying of the plague.

The king knew he was at death's door. That was why he wrote this message. And gave it to his most trusted knight to deliver to the nobleman who governed Aigues-Mortes.

The king had a precious secret to reveal. And a royal command to give.

The secret was precious indeed. It was made of gold and studded with rare jewels that surrounded the largest emerald the king had ever seen. It was a crown, which Louis IX wished now he had never seen.

The king had come upon the crown after his first Crusade had ended in his being taken prisoner. It had taken him years to raise the ransom for his release. But he had not abandoned his dream of someday defeating the Moslems. For two more years he stayed in Egypt to build defenses for land that had been won by Crusaders. There one night he raided the camp of a tribe of wandering people said to be thieves. And he discovered the crown.

The crown belonged to this people. Louis IX had found it on a man who lay wounded and dying, doubtless their king. This man had warned Louis not to take it. He had spoken of a curse that would wreak revenge on anyone who stole it. But Louis had not believed him. Why take the word of the leader of a gang of thieves? Especially when Louis could put the crown to good use. He would store it away in France and hold it in reserve. If he was captured when he launched his next Crusade, he'd have a king's ransom to pay for his freedom.

Now Louis IX saw his mistake—too late. No amount of wealth would release him from the prison he was going to. Not even a priceless crown would rescue him from the grave. As he lay on his deathbed the best he could do was save those who came after him from the curse that was taking revenge on him.

He ordered his man in Aigues-Mortes to give back the crown to its rightful owners. Some of the tribe had entered France, and could return it to their ruler. Louis IX did not know what they called themselves. They spoke a tongue no one else understood. But the French had given them a name. *Gitans*.

That was the end of the king's story. All he had to add was where to find the crown. He told where he had hidden it. And drew a picture to make sure it could be found.

Sarah was the first to break the silence in the hut. "The crown of the Rom! It is real," she said in a voice filled with awe.

The voice of the man in the iron mask was gleeful. "It is real—and it is mine!"

Chapter 12

The moon was a pale sliver hanging over Aigues-Mortes. Stars studded the sky with dazzling pinpoints of light. But the town itself was pitch-dark. The local citizens went to bed early. And they did not waste money on lamps for empty streets.

There was no one awake to see the flashlights of the group moving through the darkness. No one to wonder what brought together an American man, an American boy, a beautiful dark-haired girl, two brutal gunmen, and—the strangest sight of all—a man all in black, wearing an iron mask.

"Read the directions, Mr. Thornton," the man ordered. "Be careful not to get them wrong. The Gypsy girl will be the first to pay for a mistake."

"First we must find the Constance Tower," Thorn said, consulting the manuscript.

"That is easy," the man in the iron mask said. "This way."

The Constance Tower was by far the largest building in town. Round and tall, it stood like a giant cylinder in one corner of the town walls.

It was made of thick stone, with no window openings near the ground. Its only entrance was a thick oaken door.

The man in the iron mask tried it.

"Locked, of course," he muttered. "These local villagers keep everything under lock and key. Still, it will be easy to open."

He pounded his fist against the door. From inside, a voice said something indistinct. Then the door opened a crack.

The man in the iron mask immediately shoved it open violently. He didn't have to tell his gunmen what to do. One of them moved quickly through the doorway. There was the sickening thump of a gun barrel against a skull.

The man in the iron mask entered. He let his flashlight play for a moment on the stone floor. A white-haired watchman in a gray nightshirt lay crumpled there.

"See how easy it is to get things done," he remarked. "Now, Mr. Thornton, make it easy on yourself and your friends. Lead me to the crown without delay."

Thorn studied the manuscript. "We climb to the fourth floor of the tower," he said.

The gunmen bound and gagged the unconscious watchman. Then the group went up winding stone stairs to the fourth floor.

They found themselves in a round stone room. There was no furniture, and the only breaks in the stone walls were narrow slits. This tower was designed not for gracious living but for defense to the death.

"Now we must count flowers," said Thorn after another look at the manuscript.

"What flowers?" demanded the man in the iron mask. "There have been no flowers here for six hundred years."

"Here's one of them," said Indy. He pointed to where the flashlight shone on a flower carved in stone. The stone flower was embedded in the wall. The man in the mask shone his flashlight around the room. A circle of the same kind of stone flowers ringed the whole room.

"Ah yes, the most beautiful flower in the world," said the man in the iron mask. His voice was unexpectedly gentle as he looked at the three-petaled flower.

Who'd have figured this guy for a flower lover? thought Indy.

"What kind of flower is it?" Indy asked, trying to understand what moved the man.

"An iris," said the man in the iron mask, his voice reverent. "A royal iris. It is the symbol of the kings of France—the fleur-de-lys."

Thorn's voice cut in. "According to the picture the king drew, we are to count nine flowers around the room, starting at the right of the entrance."

"That picture must have been what I thought was a map," said Indy, his eyes lighting up. "A treasure map. Remember, when I got that first quick look at the manu-script? It looks like I was right about the treasure part, anyway. What did you call my idea, Thorn? A 'romantic notion,' right?"

Despite the spot they were in, Indy did have the satisfaction of hearing Thorn say, "Okay. You were right and I was wrong." He even smiled a little. "Maybe the world is a more romantic place than I thought. Any-way, we'll soon see."

"*Very* soon," said the man in the iron mask, his voice charged with excitement.

Counting quickly, they reached the ninth flower.

"Now what?" the man in the iron mask demanded.

"We'll see if I've figured out the king's second picture correctly," Thorn said. "Hold the flashlight steady on the flower."

As the man did so Thorn placed his fin-gers on the central upright petal of the fleur-de-lys. He pushed. Nothing happened.

"Is this some kind of joke?" the man in the iron mask snarled. "See if you can laugh when we get finished with your Gypsy friend."

He nodded to one of his gunmen. The gunman pressed a pistol against Sarah's head. She refused to plead for mercy. But she could not stop herself from trembling.

"No! Wait!" Thorn said. His face was pale. "It must be stiff with age. Let me try again."

He pushed again, this time harder. Still, nothing happened.

He pushed even harder. A vein stood out on his forehead. Sweat beaded his face.

There was a sound. A very faint sound. It was an unmistakable creaking.

"It's moving!" Thorn exclaimed triumphantly.

At first slowly, then faster, the stone flower moved inward. There was a muffled click. Then a section of the stone wall about a yard square swung inward on a concealed hinge.

The man in the iron mask beamed his flashlight into the opening.

The light struck the dazzling gold of a crown that lay within arm's reach. Indy blinked, and then made out the eerie green glow of an emerald set in the crown. The emerald was enormous, dwarfing the diamonds and rubies around it.

"The crown! At last!" exclaimed the man in the iron mask.

His eager hand moved toward the opening.

But suddenly he stopped.

"I am forgetting my manners," he said, turning to Indy. "I must not be selfish. You were so quick to guess there was a treasure. Let me give you a reward. You can be the first to have the pleasure of holding it. Please, be my guest."

Indy shrugged. This guy was truly weird. But why argue? Quickly he reached into the opening, curled his fingers over the crown, and started to lift it.

Then he froze as Thorn shouted, *"No, Indy, don't!"*

Chapter 13

Fortunately, Thorn did more than shout. Indy's fingers flew open as Thorn's hands grabbed his shoulders and violently jerked him backward.

Indy's mouth flew open too. Then it closed as he gave a giant gulp.

A massive blade had dropped down in the opening. It landed with a loud thud where Indy's wrist had been a heartbeat before.

Indy heard his own heart thudding as he stared at it.

Then he heard the man in the iron mask chuckling.

"Ah, Mr. Thornton, was there something in the manuscript that you forgot to translate for me?" he said. "A warning about a device guarding the crown from thieves? Such devices were often used, I believe. And I'm sure the king did not want his own people to have their hands chopped off."

Thorn said nothing. He glumly watched the man in the iron mask reach over the blade and lift out the crown.

"Thank you for your help, anyway," the man said. "Such a shame your reward will have to be so unpleasant. The best I can do is make it as painless as possible."

"But you will release Sarah," Thorn said. "You promised."

"Did I?" the man said. "One says so many things in the heat of the moment. You can't expect me to remember all of them."

"But— You can't— Where is your sense of—" Thorn sputtered, his voice choked with outrage.

"It's no use," Sarah said, putting her hand on his arm. "I knew I could not expect mercy from this man. I'm sorry for pretending to think you could save me. But I wanted you to agree to lead the way to the crown. I promised my great-grandfather to try to bring it to light, no matter what. A Rom cannot break a promise like that."

"You Gypsies have such quaint ways," said the man in the mask. "I suppose you will now threaten me with a curse if I harm you."

"I won't waste my breath," Sarah said. "If you do not believe what the king wrote about the revenge of the crown, I know you will not listen to me."

"Yes, don't waste your breath," said the man. "Especially when you have so few breaths left before you breathe your last."

Indy found it hard to breathe at all. How did the man in the iron mask plan to get rid of them? And when? Actually, Indy was in no hurry to find out.

"Come, let us be going," said the man. "We have a long ride ahead of us before we reach our destination—and you reach your last stop."

He and his men herded Indy, Thorn, and Sarah out of the tower. They went back through the dark, deserted streets to the two cars.

Just before the man in the iron mask got into his limousine, he said, "There is one promise I will keep. I will make your deaths painless. But I won't say more. You can amuse yourself during your car ride trying to guess how you will meet your ends."

Indy, Thorn, and Sarah didn't try to guess—not out loud, anyway. They sat silently under the gun of a guard as their car rolled through the night. Indy kept trying to see a way out of this trap. From the intent eyes of the others, they were too. But they didn't look as if they were having any luck. Their faces were as bleak as the scene that the first light of dawn revealed.

They were driving through a wasteland of soot-covered factories and flimsy wooden shacks with straggly gardens. They still had no hint of what awaited them. But at least Sarah now could say where they were. "We're entering Marseilles."

"Strange," mused Thorn. "You'd think he'd take us to an isolated spot. Marseilles is the third-largest city in France."

"Not so strange, if you know Marseilles," Sarah said. "There's a section of the city called the old port. It's a maze of old buildings and narrow, crooked streets. Even policemen don't go in there alone. It's a criminal's paradise—a kingdom of crooks."

The car turned onto a wide avenue sloping downward. At its end Indy could see the masts of fishing boats crowding the harbor.

"I was right," Sarah said. "We're on the Canebière—the main street of the city. It leads to the old port."

Minutes later, the car was squeezing through a narrow side street. Carts loaded with vegetables and others stacked with fish made way for it. Men staggering out of all-night cafés pressed against grimy walls when they heard its horn blasts.

The car braked before a large wooden gate. The horn sounded three long blasts, two short ones, and the gate opened. The car rolled in, and two men closed the gate behind it.

Indy stared out the car window. They were in a huge courtyard. The limousine was already parked there. The man in the iron mask had made much better time than they had.

No doubt he was waiting for them inside the building that rose before them—a building that made Indy's eyes widen with amazement.

From the street, the structure had seemed ordinary. It was a good deal higher than its neighbors, but just as shabby.

But in the courtyard, Indy stared at a building that was a picture of elegance. Its stone walls were free of grime. Its rows of windows were sparkling bright. Broad marble steps led up to a gleaming oak door flanked by marble columns.

It was a stunning sight. For a moment, Indy forgot his fear as he gazed at it. "It looks like a palace," he said. "If this part of town is a kingdom of crooks, this guy has to be some kind of king."

The servant who answered the purple velvet door pull backed up Indy's hunch. He wore a red velvet coat with silver brocade, and tight white breeches. On his head was a white powdered wig, tied back with a black velvet ribbon.

"He's right out of the eighteenth century,"

said Thorn. He, too, had momentarily forgotten his fear in the wonder of this mysterious mansion.

"Welcome to my home," said a voice from the end of the entranceway. It was the man in the iron mask. Indy was disappointed to see that the man's face was still covered. Indy was hoping to get a look at him.

No luck. What the man in the iron mask wanted to show them was his home.

"It is a sight you should really see—before you die," he said.

His words were like a slap, bringing his prisoners back to the desperate spot they were in. Indy and Thorn both winced, and Sarah's hand reached out to tighten around Thorn's.

With the gunmen's weapons trained on them, they followed the man through room after room, floor after floor. The furniture would have filled a hundred expensive antique stores. And there were crystal chandeliers, richly colored carpets on marble floors, golden harps, and gilded harpsichords. Huge paintings full of romping shepherds and shepherdesses hung on walls covered in velvet and silk.

"It hardly seems real," said Sarah.

"It's like a trip through time," said Thorn, shaking his head in amazement at the splendor surrounding them.

"I just wonder what it's leading up to," said Indy, glancing at the glinting guns in their guards' hands and the gleam in the eyes of their boss.

"But I don't want to bore you," the man in the mask said at last. "I know how impatient you must be to view the fate I promised you. Come see it now."

He opened a door and ushered them into a large room. It was on the top floor, and morning light flooded through its large windows. The light shone on the object in the center of the marble floor.

Indy stared at it. He saw a wooden frame. In the bottom part was a place to rest your neck. Above was a massive blade, which a pull of a cord would release. The blade would come down. And your head would drop into a basket thoughtfully placed in front. Very simple. Very effective.

"You see, I will keep my promise to you," declared the man. "This was invented by a kindly doctor to make death as painless as possible. A grateful France named it after him. What a great man he was. Dr. Guillotin."

Chapter 14

Indy had heard of the guillotine. It was an instrument of death first used in the French Revolution over a century before, and it was still used by French law to carry out death sentences. He had never seen one until now. It was a sight he could have done without.

Indy swallowed hard. Instinctively he touched his throat. He looked away.

For the first time, he noticed that the room was lined with full-length portraits—portraits of men wearing crowns.

He heard the man in the iron mask say, "I hope you like my little toy. I went to great trouble getting it. It is a genuine antique.

During the Revolution, it removed the heads of the greatest aristocrats in France."

"Like those guys up there?" said Indy, indicating the portraits.

"Those men were not mere aristocrats," the man in the iron mask said indignantly. "They were the kings of France. Every one of them, from the first onward."

There was a note of reverence in the man's voice. Funny, Indy thought. You wouldn't figure a crook to be so patriotic.

As if reading Indy's mind, the man went on, "You must be wondering why I have these portraits. I feel I should tell you all— especially you, Mr. Thornton. As a historian, you will be able to appreciate it."

The man in the mask led them to a window. High above the other buildings, it provided a fine view of the harbor.

"Do you see that small island?" he said.

Indy, Sarah, and Thorn nodded. On the horizon of the harbor was a small landmass, with a walled building on it.

"That is the Château d'If," the man in the iron mask told them. "A fortress that once held France's most important prisoners."

Suddenly Thorn clapped his hand to his forehead. "Of course! Why didn't I think of it before!" he exclaimed. "The man in the iron mask."

Indy and Sarah gave him a puzzled look.

The man in the iron mask sounded pleased. "I see you know the story."

"Naturally. It's well known," said Thorn.

"Why not tell your friends?" the man suggested. His chuckle sounded like a cackle. "I'm sure they're *dying* to know."

Thorn grimaced. Nonetheless, he turned to Indy and Sarah. "Centuries ago, a mysterious prisoner was held in the Château d'If for over forty years. No one ever saw his face. It was covered by an iron mask." Thorn looked at the present man in the iron mask. "Is there a connection?"

"Finish the story and I will tell you," the man in the iron mask said.

Thorn shrugged. "There's nothing more to tell. No one ever found out who the man was."

"Really?" the man asked.

"Oh, there were wild rumors," Thorn said. "There was even one fairy tale that said he was the twin brother of King Louis the Fourteenth. Supposedly, he was held captive for life so that he couldn't claim the throne."

"It was no fairy story," the man in the iron mask declared in a voice like steel. "It was the truth. The royal blood of France flowed in his veins. Just as it flows in mine *Look!*"

With a sudden gesture, the man took off his mask.

The prisoners stared at his face. Then at one another.

"Do you see what I see?" said Indy.

"Impossible," said Thorn, but weakly.

"It's true," said Sarah, her eyes moving from the man's face to the faces in the portraits on the wall.

The resemblance was unmistakable. The man had the same distinctly sheeplike face as the kings of France. All of them looked as if they would say "Baa" when they talked.

"Of course it's true," the man gloated. "And now I will tell you the rest of the truth—since you will not be around when I reveal it to the world. Before he was shut away, the man in the iron mask had a secret child.

That child was raised knowing what his rightful place was. So was his child after him. And so on until today. Loyal retainers always served and protected them as they waited for the right time to come. Now it has. Now the last descendant of the man in the iron mask will claim his birthright." The man paused, then boomed out, *"I will be crowned king of France."*

Before he could stop himself, Indy blurted out, "That's crazy. They don't *have* kings here anymore!"

But the man was not enraged. He laughed. "Crazy, is it? Tell that to the German kaiser. He is willing to help a fellow king regain control of France. Already he is planning a war that will destroy our present government and rid Europe of the foolish notion of people voting for their leaders. He has all but promised to restore me to the throne, and the gift I have for him now will seal the bargain." The man gazed fondly at the Gypsy crown, now resting on a marble table. "The kaiser is a childish fellow, really. It's only natural, considering how young his dynasty is, compared to mine. He longs for trinkets to rival the crown jewels of England. *This* will earn his undying gratitude."

"Then you don't want the crown for yourself?" said Indy.

"Hardly," the man said with contempt. "A Gypsy crown is nothing, compared to the crown of France. That is the crown I will wear when I stand here in this room and send the pitiful leaders of the present government to their fates. My ancestors will watch the same guillotine that began the disgusting rule of common people finally end it."

A fresh smile broke out on his face. A smile that made Indy shiver.

"I have a wonderful idea," the man said, his eyes lighting up. "I will make this a dress rehearsal of that glorious day." He turned to his men. "I will put on this crown and pass sentence on the prisoners. As soon as I do let the guillotine do its work."

Smiling even more, he added, "We will follow the old rule. Women and children first."

With that last bad joke, the man lifted the Gypsy crown, and Sarah and Indy and Thorn waited for death to descend.

Chapter 15

The would-be king stood poised, the crown high above his head, a satisfied smile on his face. In an instant it would be all over.

Got to stop him, Indy thought, got to buy time.

"Wait a minute," Indy said.

"Why should I?" the man asked, still holding the crown above his head.

"You haven't told us everything," Indy said desperately. "If I have to go, I don't want to go with a lot of questions about you I can't answer."

It worked. The man lowered the crown. As

Indy figured, he couldn't resist talking about himself a little longer.

"What do you want to know?" he asked.

Indy's brain whirred furiously. "How did you know about the crown—and the manuscript?" was the best he could come up with.

It was enough.

"The heirs of Louis the Ninth had heard about the crown," the man explained, "just as they had heard about his mysterious lost last message. They searched for both in vain. It became a family secret passed down from generation to generation. On my side of the family as well as the other. So when one of my people heard about Monsieur Dupont's find, I knew at once what it could mean."

"But why didn't you just grab the manuscript from him then?" Indy asked. Keep him talking, he thought.

"I did not know where he had hidden it," the man replied. "We could have tried to make him talk. But it was much easier and surer to wait for you Americans to pick the manuscript up and then take it from you. Does that answer your question?"

"One other thing I don't get," Indy went on frantically. He was running out of questions. "Where do you get all your money? This place has to cost a fortune. Plus the payroll for your men."

The man shrugged. "My ancestors decided if they had to wait to become kings of France, they would become kings of a different kind. My family has ruled the Marseilles underworld for over a century."

"But why the business with the iron mask?" Indy continued.

"The male heads of my family have always worn it," the man explained. He looked fondly at the mask now lying at his feet. "It is a sign of respect for our ancestor. And a way to keep our royal faces hidden from outsiders until our time of triumph arrives. And now, if there are no more questions . . ."

Indy opened his mouth, hoping something would come out.

But before it did, he was horrified to hear Sarah say, "Enough of this game of cat and mouse. Put that silly crown on your head and get this over with."

The man glowered at her. He said in an

icy voice, "Always happy to oblige a lady." Then he repeated, "Women and children first."

With that, he firmly placed the crown upon his head. As he did so, his mouth opened to pronounce the death sentence.

What came out was a horrible scream.

He stood frozen for a moment, as if a shock had passed through his body. Then he collapsed in a heap on the floor.

It was everyone else's turn to stand frozen.

Everyone but Sarah.

She had moved like lightning even before the man fell. As he hit the floor she scooped up the crown from his limp hand. Then she reached down, unbuckled and whipped off his belt. All this was done so fast that Indy barely had time to blink, much less wonder what she was doing with the belt.

"Quick! Come on!" she yelled to Indy and Thorn as she sped past them, the crown in one hand, the belt in the other.

That was enough to get them moving faster than the guards. Indy and Thorn raced out of the room and down the stairs after Sarah.

But the guards had snapped out of shock too. They pounded after the fleeing threesome.

Indy and the others reached the ground floor, ran out the door and through the courtyard. The guards at the gate were sitting drinking coffee when they dashed by. The coffee cups smashed to the ground as the guards jumped up and joined the chase.

Indy had hoped that out on the street they would be safe. He saw how wrong he was. The guards kept after them. And he remembered what Sarah had said—crime ruled this neighborhood. They wouldn't be home free until they made it out of the old port.

It looked as though they would make it. He and Thorn and Sarah were running abreast, well ahead of the crooks. Thorn was actually grinning. Then Indy saw why. Thorn triumphantly waved the manuscript in his hand. He must have spied it lying unattended as they dashed through the house. Trust Thorn to keep on the lookout for something like that.

Meanwhile, the local citizens didn't seem surprised by the chase. They were interested in only one thing—keeping out of the way.

Then it happened—on a street lined with food stalls. Sarah gave a shriek as her feet flew out from under her. An overripe tomato on the cobblestones had sent her flying.

Indy and Thorn were five feet ahead of her before they could stop. They turned back to help her.

Indy's stomach sank. He saw they were too late. The guards were almost upon her.

Sarah saw it too.

"Forget me!" she shouted. "Save the crown!"

On her knees, she threw it to Thorn.

He caught it. But he handed it to Indy, along with the manuscript.

"Keep them safe," Thorn said. Indy stood with his hands full, his eyes unable to believe what they were seeing, as Thorn charged.

One guard already had a grip on Sarah. Thorn's hand chopped against the back of the man's head, and the man collapsed like a popped balloon. By then, another guard was leaping on Thorn's back. Thorn wheeled, and suddenly the man flew through the air and crashed against a wall. Another guard reached Thorn, and a moment later was screaming with pain as his arm bone snapped sickeningly. Yet another one collapsed unconscious when the top of Thorn's head met the man's forehead with a loud crack.

Indy couldn't resist joining in. He laid down the crown and manuscript and picked up a long pole draped with hundreds of garlic heads. He broke it over the head of one charging guard. The next thing he grabbed was a bottle of wine. It exploded in a shower of red on the head of another.

Sarah was on her feet with a weapon of her own. She swung the belt in her hand at the head of the last crook. It landed with a loud clunk, and he landed in a heap.

"I once did quite a good research paper on Oriental methods of unarmed conflict," Thornton explained as they surveyed the k.o.'d crooks littering the street. "That was a long time ago, of course. But it's amazing how things come back to you." Then he looked into Sarah's eyes. "Especially when you want to help someone you care for very, very much."

Meanwhile, Indy was thinking up a new nickname for Thornton N. Thornton VI.

Thorn didn't seem right anymore.

TNT seemed a lot better.

Then, suddenly, TNT looked away from Sarah and at Indy. TNT's smile faded.

"*Indy*," he said. "Where're the crown and the manuscript."

"Right there, where I left—" Indy got no farther.

His eyes had reached the spot where he had laid down the precious objects.

They were gone!

Chapter 16

Indy turned away, sick at heart. "I'm sorry," he said to Sarah and TNT. "I figured you needed my help. I forgot where we were. This neighborhood must be a den of thieves."

TNT and Sarah looked back at him bleakly, not knowing what to say.

"Monsieur," a woman's voice said.

They turned to see an old woman in black emerging from behind a cart heaped high with shiny purple eggplants. She held the crown and the manuscript.

She gave them to TNT, a toothless smile creasing her wrinkled face. She spoke to him in French, and a smile lit his face, as if she

114

had said something very funny. Then he thanked her warmly.

"What did she say to you?" Indy asked him as they headed out of the old port.

"She picked them up for safekeeping," TNT answered. "She warned us to be more careful. She said there are a lot of thieving Gypsies around."

Indy shook his head. "I guess there's no escaping prejudice. Here I thought the people in this neighborhood were all thieves. And the old woman had the usual feeling about Gypsies. I can see it's something you always have to guard against."

"You have to keep a sharp eye out for it," TNT agreed.

When he said that, Indy noticed something. "Thornton, what happened to your glasses?"

"They got knocked off," Thorn said.

"Do you have another pair?" Sarah asked, looking concerned.

"I'm afraid not," TNT said.

"We will have to get you some new ones," said Sarah. "Perhaps we can find a shop that does fast work."

TNT looked a bit embarrassed. "Actually, I don't need them. Their lenses were window glass. I wore them because I thought they would help me in my profession. They would make me look older . . . more scholarly . . . more . . ."

"Stuffy?" Indy suggested.

TNT grinned. "I guess that's the word."

"You look great without them," Indy said. He meant it. TNT might look much younger than before, but he looked a lot more *real*.

"I agree," said Sarah, and she reached up and gently touched TNT's face where the glasses had been. Then she said, "Since we don't have to stop to get glasses, we can go straight back to Saintes-Maries. We can take a taxi."

TNT shook his head. "The crooks lifted all my cash. We can't afford the fare."

"Yes, we can," Sarah said. She showed them the belt she had taken off the would-be king. The same belt she had used to knock out the last crook. Indy saw why it had landed with such a loud clunk.

It was a money belt, bulging with gold coins.

"I thought he would be wearing one," Sarah explained. "He might pretend to be a king, but he was still a Frenchman. They like to keep their money close to them. From what this belt weighs, it holds all the gold you paid Monsieur Dupont. And then some."

"Good thinking," said TNT. His eyes shone with admiration. "Fast thinking, too. If you hadn't moved when you did, we never would have gotten out of that house alive."

"Right," Indy agreed. "It was like you knew what was going to happen."

Sarah said nothing. She simply turned the crown upside down so they could see inside. Then she pressed down on the bottom of its inner rim. Suddenly a steel needle shot inward from the rim, then retreated back to its hiding place.

"I see how it works," Indy said. "Anybody putting on the crown triggers the needle."

"Unless you know how to turn the device off beforehand," Sarah said.

"Then you knew what would happen to the man if he put the crown on," Indy said.

Sarah nodded. "I tried not to look at his head when I grabbed the crown."

"But how did you know?" TNT asked.

Sarah smiled. "That man wasn't the only one with a family that passed down knowledge about the crown from generation to generation. And my family knew far more than his. We were the ones who had it made. Just as we are the ones who have spent hundreds of years trying to get it back."

"Sarah, I've been thinking, and—" TNT began. Then he paused and said, "But we can talk it over on the taxi ride."

When they found a taxi, TNT asked Indy to sit in the front seat. There were things he wanted to discuss with Sarah—in private.

Indy spent the taxi ride trying to ignore the smell of garlic from the driver beside him, and trying to hear the conversation behind him. The rumbling motor kept him from catching a word. But in the rearview mirror he could see TNT and Sarah talking non-stop. He could also see that somewhere along the line, they had started holding hands.

Dusk was descending on the Gypsy encampment when they arrived. They got out of the taxi. But instead of paying the driver,

Sarah spoke a few words in French to him. He shrugged, and sat in his cab waiting.

They walked out of earshot of the taxi. Then TNT stopped and said, "Indiana, I have something to tell you."

"I kind of figured that," Indy said.

"I've decided to return the crown to Sarah's great-grandfather," TNT said. "She's convinced me it is rightfully his. That far outweighs its value to scholars. I'm sure your father will go along with that."

"The manuscript is all he's interested in," Indy agreed. "Jewels and stuff don't mean much to him. Of course, he won't mind getting his money back. Getting things cheap is one of his favorite activities."

"One more thing," TNT said. "I'd like you to convince him to go along with the story that the crown mentioned in the manuscript turned out to be missing. We can say that over the centuries, thieves must have found it. I don't think the Gypsies would want publicity about it."

Indy was puzzled. "Why should *I* convince him? He'd listen to you before me."

Thorn cleared his throat. "I won't be going back to America with you. The Gypsies need a serious scholar to study their culture. There are so many false beliefs about them. And such little real knowledge. Even their language is unknown to outsiders."

"But what makes you think they'll let you in on any of their secrets?" Indy asked. "After all, to them you're a gorgio."

TNT cleared his throat again. "Sarah has kindly volunteered to vouch for me. And to help me with my research."

Sarah smiled. "Of course, I have warned Thornton what a big job he has ahead of him. It could take a long time. A whole lifetime."

Once again TNT's and Sarah's hands joined as their eyes met.

"No problem" said Indy. "I'll square things with my dad. But Sarah, can you do me a favor before I go?"

"Of course," Sarah said. "What is it?"

"Read Thornton's palm again," Indy requested. "I'd like to know what his future is now."

Nodding, Sarah turned TNT's hand palm up. Her dark eyes grew wide.

"How strange," she said. "I have never seen anything like this."

"Bad news?" said TNT, concerned.

"Not at all," Sarah replied, still gazing at his palm. "Since I looked at your palm last, lines have appeared on it. Many lines. And more are about to emerge. It is no longer the palm of a baby. It is the palm of a man. A man whose future is still developing. A man whose future will be very, very interesting."

"I can believe that," said Thorn, smiling at her.

"So can I," Indy said, grinning. "So can I."

HISTORICAL NOTES

The gypsies, or Rom, or Romanies, or Romanichels, are believed by many to have their origins in India. This, however, is far from certain, like so many other things about them. What is certain is that they continue to follow their wandering ways throughout the world, including the United States, despite the efforts of authorities to have them settle down. Their language, Romany, remains unknown to any but them. And they persist in denying the existence of any king among them, though rumors about one persist as well.

The story of the man in the iron mask is also a subject of controversy among scholars. There is solid evidence that such a man was indeed imprisoned in the Château d'If until his death. But the legend that he was the twin brother of King Louis XIV has never been definitely proved, though the nineteenth-century French writer Alexandre Dumas, the elder, used it as the basis for his novel *The Man in the Iron Mask*.

The old port of Marseilles was completely leveled by the occupying German army in World War II, since this haven for criminals had become a haven as well for French underground fighters against the Nazi invaders. The neighborhood, rebuilt after the war, is now a respectable part of the city.

Unfortunately for our knowledge of Gypsy culture, Thornton N. Thornton VI published none of his findings. In fact, he never appeared in the world of scholarship again. This came as a great surprise and considerable disappointment to Professor Henry Jones. But not to Henry Jones, Junior, a.k.a. Indy.

TO FIND OUT MORE, CHECK OUT . . .

Gypsies by Howard Greenfeld. Published by Crown Books, 1977. Discover the mysteries of the gypsy world in this fascinating book about gypsy life and traditions throughout the centuries—and learn more about how Rom like Sarah and her family lived. Photographs.

Penengro by Hilda van Stockum. Published by Farrar, Straus & Giroux, 1972. In this story an orphan boy experiences gypsy life firsthand when he is befriended by gypsies and goes to live with them. Illustrations by the author.

Living in a Crusader Land by R. J. Unstead. Published by Addison-Wesley, 1973. Journey to the Holy Land with the Crusaders and see how and why European knights battled Arabs, Turks, and others for over 200 years. The details of battle and descriptions of Jerusalem will help you picture Louis IX on his long adventure and imagine how the knights dressed. Illustrations by Victor Ambrus.

"The Camargue, Land of Cowboys and Gypsies," by Eugene L. Kammerman. Published in *National Geographic*, May 1956. A look at the exciting Camargue region of France, where Indy and Thorn traveled. Gypsy traditions, bullfighting, maps, and a spectacular photo of the walls of Aigues-Mortes, just as Indy would have seen them! Color photographs.

The Man in the Iron Mask by Alexandre Dumas. In this classic French novel, first published around 1850, the twin brother of King Louis XIV is imprisoned for life and condemned to wear an iron mask. This is the legend our Man in the Iron Mask tells to Indy, Thorn, and Sarah. Available in many English-language editions, including one published by Airmont in 1967. Fantastic reading, at about the ninth-grade level.

SHARE THE ADVENTURE!